Brown Bear Wood

If You Go Down to the Woods Today

Poems by
Rachel Piercey

Illustrated by
Freya Hartas

MAGIC CAT PUBLISHING

NEW YORK

The illustrations were drawn in pencil and colored digitally.
Set in Bentham, La Parisienne, Lancelot, and Sevillana.

Library of Congress Control Number 2020943633
ISBN 978-1-4197-5158-5

Text © 2021 Rachel Piercey
Illustrations © 2021 Freya Hartas
"Teddy Bears Picnic" Words and Music by John W Bratton, Jimmy Kennedy © 1932,
Reproduced by permission of B Feldman & Co Ltd, M Witmark & Sons & EMI Music Publishing, London W1F 9LD
Cover © Magic Cat 2021
Book design by Nicola Price

Printed and bound in China
10 9 8 7 6 5 4 3 2 1

ABRAMS The Art of Books
195 Broadway, New York, NY 10007
abramsbooks.com

Hello! I'm Bear! Can we be friends?

I'd love it if we could.

Perhaps you'd like to see my home,

the world inside the woods?

SPRING BRINGS NEW LIFE
BEAR'S WORLD AWAKES

Spring is waking up the world!
Will you come with me?
My woodland home is full of friends,
let's peek inside and see . . .

The winter months were long and cold,
the ground was hard with ice.
But now the grassy floor's alive
with rabbits, deer, and mice.

We've woken up to gold and green,
the air is smelling sweet.
We're starting to explore again,
to stretch our tails and feet.

My woodland's full of animals,
of every different kind.
So shall we stay here for a while
and see what we can find?

What to spot in Bear's world

- **BEAR** wandering the woods
- **SKUNK** snoozing under a bush
- **BLUEBELLS** pushing up their heads
- **BABY CHIPMUNK** in a hammock
- **SNAKE** enjoying the spring air
- **BLUE TITS** building their nest
- **PROFESSOR OWL** trying to sleep
- **RED ADMIRAL BUTTERFLY** sipping nectar
- **MAMA WEASEL** wheeling a wheelbarrow
- Two **BIRDS** returning from their winter break
- Five brown **BABY MICE**, many ready to explore
- Two **CATERPILLARS** saying hello
- **GREY SQUIRREL** swinging through the air with a friend!

HOME SWEET HOME

All of us are busy now,
settling into home:
bringing, building, burrowing,
and making it our own.

A tree for Owl, a log for Frog,
a web for spinning Spider,
a hole dug from the earth for Fox,
her rusty cubs beside her.

Each tree can host a hundred rooms,
with roots to hide beneath,
with hidey-holes inside the bark,
and boughs where creatures sleep.

And everywhere the sun and sky
grow from the ground as well,
in dazzling yellow daffodils,
in blue and breezy bells.

What to spot near Bear's home

BEAR decorating his den with beautiful flowers from the woodland

WEASEL poking her head out of a log

MAMA WREN and **PAPA WREN** gathering sticks to build their nest

SPIDER spinning a special sign

A **FOX CUB** who has gone wandering

FROG dusting his home

ANT climbing a staircase

GRANDMA BAT and GRANDPA BAT resting upside-down

RACCOON's leaf-lined bed

MOUSE riding piggyback

BUNNIES sweeping the entrance

RED and GREY SQUIRRELS zipping down a tree-root slide

PAPA BEAR collecting flowers

Four NESTS full of eggs

FAWNS watering some bluebells

RED ADMIRAL BUTTERFLY on MAMA DEER's velvety nose

SCHOOL DAYS

It's time for school inside the woods,
to come and learn together,
and make a whole new group of friends
with fur or shells or feathers.

Our classroom is a hollow trunk,
our playground is close by.
Our teachers pad from underground
or dart in from the sky.

We learn the moon, we feel the sun,
we read the changing trees,
we keep a record of the pond,
make music from the breeze.

And all the different animals
look after one another:
new-to-school, or oldest-here,
neighbors, sisters, brothers.

LEAVES

BRANCHES

NEST

TRUNK

ROOTS

SWEET PEAS

CABBAGES

POTATOES

What to spot at school

- **BEAR** reciting poetry to his classmates
- **MAMA SQUIRREL** teaching the animals how to count
- **PROFESSOR OWL** giving a lesson on the moon
- A lively game of **HOPSCOTCH**
- **SPARROW** leading a chirping, cheeping choir
- **SPIDER** teaching the alphabet
- Three **CATERPILLARS** looking at leaves *very* closely
- A **NEW STUDENT**, here for the summer months, being made welcome
- A **WOODLAND MAP**
- Four **WOODPECKER CHICKS** listening in from home
- A **VEGETABLE PATCH**
- **NANA RABBIT** helping the students make wind chimes
- **FROG** teaching a science lesson by the pond

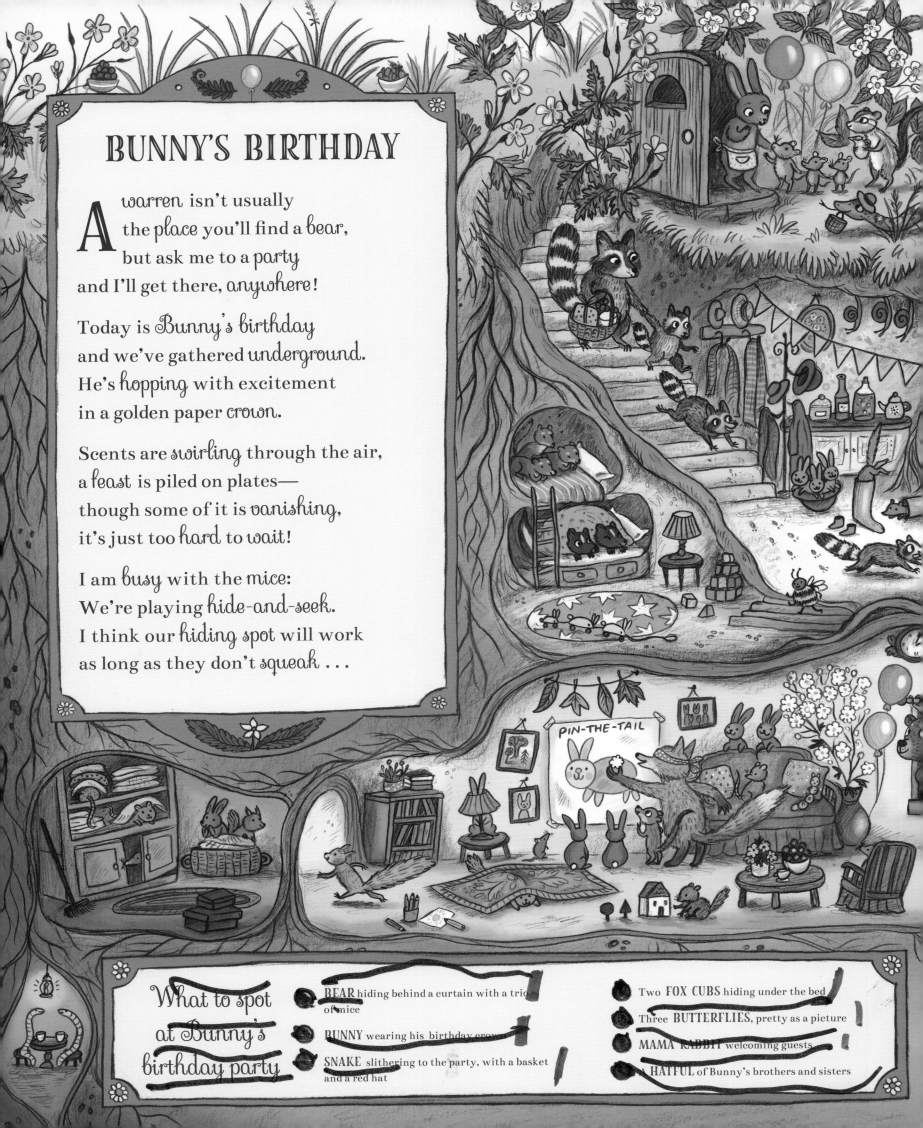

BUNNY'S BIRTHDAY

A warren isn't usually
the place you'll find a bear,
but ask me to a party
and I'll get there, anywhere!

Today is Bunny's birthday
and we've gathered underground.
He's hopping with excitement
in a golden paper crown.

Scents are swirling through the air,
a feast is piled on plates—
though some of it is vanishing,
it's just too hard to wait!

I am busy with the mice:
We're playing hide-and-seek.
I think our hiding spot will work
as long as they don't squeak . . .

PIN-THE-TAIL

What to spot at Bunny's birthday party

- BEAR hiding behind a curtain with a trio of mice
- BUNNY wearing his birthday crown
- SNAKE slithering to the party, with a basket and a red hat

- Two FOX CUBS hiding under the bed
- Three BUTTERFLIES, pretty as a picture
- MAMA RABBIT welcoming guests
- A HATFUL of Bunny's brothers and sisters

NANA RABBIT putting the finishing touches on the birthday cake

A pile of PRESENTS and CARDS

A game of PIN-THE-TAIL on the bunny

Three topsy-turvy SNAILS

Two BABY WEASELS wriggling into rainboots

A plate of wibbly-wobbly JELL-O

PAPA RABBIT pinning up bunting

Two bouncing BEES

Shelves of yellow CHICKS

SUMMER BRINGS THE SUN
FIELD DAY

The days are long and balmy now,
the sun climbs higher and higher.
Trees are thick with glossy leaves,
like flicks of emerald fire.

And what a perfect day for sport:
for races up and down,
and back and forth, and fast and slow,
in the air and on the ground.

From the sidelines, families watch
to clap and cheer their crew,
refreshing us with picnic treats
and cups of morning dew.

Who will win the running race?
Whose the furthest throw?
Who can jump the highest, longest?
Ready, get set, GO!

What to spot at field day

- **BEAR** stretching in a yellow bib to prepare for the games
- A **SIX-LEGGED RACE**
- A **LEAF PARACHUTE** competition
- An exciting game of **STICK THROWING**
- Pink and yellow **DOG ROSES** and **HONEYSUCKLE**
- **PICNICS**, high and low
- **TROPHIES** and **ROSETTES** on display
- A sky-high **RELAY RACE**
- Two **HIGH JUMP** competitions
- A very slow **SNAIL** and **SLUG RACE**
- **PAPA DEER** and **MAMA FOX** launching into the long jump
- A **TUG-OF-WAR** between families
- Two **WOODPECKERS** pecking the same tree, head-to-head

HIGH SUMMER

The sun is right above my head,
the air is silky warm.
The rustle-bustle bushy leaves
have many shapes and forms.

And up here there are leaping legs,
and claws that cling on tight.
And up here there are tails which trail
through dazzling, dappled light.

Just listen! You can hear the birds,
they coo and sing nearby.
Just watch! That funny-looking leaf
unfolds a butterfly.

He sunbathes on the bark a while,
enjoying his new home,
while round him, bugs and beetles crawl
and gleam like precious stones.

What to spot in high summer

- A mischievous **CATERPILLAR** tickling **BEAR**
- **GREY SQUIRRELS** playing tag
- **MAMA MOUSE** and **PAPA MOUSE** reading
- The **PIGEON FAMILY** singing for joy
- **SPIDER** spinning her lacy web
- **GRANDMA BAT** and **GRANDPA BAT** fast asleep
- **PROFESSOR OWL** having her nap interrupted
- Two smiling **RACCOONS**
- **BEAR'S LITTLE SISTER** climbing a tree
- **MICE** playing frisbee
- **BEES** performing acrobatics in the sky
- Five **LADYBUGS** on a leaf
- Three **BUTTERFLIES** emerging from their chrysalises

SWIMMING LESSONS

Welcome to our woodland pond
where dragonflies are skimming,
where willows swish and lilies glow,
and we are going swimming!

It's full of possibilities,
the water: we can glide,
or paddle, float, or make it swell,
or even dive inside.

Beneath our toes the silver fish
are gently flicking by,
while Rabbit sails a jolly boat
to keep her whiskers dry.

And on the banks, the grownups rest,
content to watch the fun,
calling out encouragement
and soaking up the sun.

What to spot during swimming lessons

- **BEAR** drying off after his swim
- A shy **FROG**
- Two **SHOALS** of **FISH**
- **PROFESSOR OWL** and **RACCOON** watching over the swimmers
- **MOUSE** dipping her toe into the water
- **FOX CUBS** playing tag
- **BEAR'S LITTLE BROTHER**, **BEAR'S LITTLE SISTER**, and **FAWNS** making waves
- **GRANDPA TOAD** watching over his grandchildren
- **MAMA FOX** and **MAMA DEER** drinking the swimming pool
- **PAPA BEAR** and **PAPA DEER** enjoying a thermos of tea
- **MAMA WEASEL**'s book club
- **MAMA RABBIT** in a captain's hat
- A diving **SQUIRREL**

BEAR'S PICNIC

Today's the kind of balmy day
     when all you want to do
     is picnic under summer skies,
as clouds drift into view.

A bag or basket, faded rug,
a favorite floppy hat,
some food, some friends, a ball or two—
you don't need more than that.

We've found ourselves a lovely spot,
with sunshine, shade, and flowers.
We've spread the rugs and spread the food,
we'll dawdle here for hours.

For picnics are the perfect place
for doing what you love:
to talk or read or snooze or play,
or all of the above!

What to spot at Bear's picnic

BEAR eating a bowl of **WILD STRAWBERRIES**

MICE and **CHIPMUNKS** playing catch

SWIMSUITS drying on a mossy log

A **FOX CUB** swinging her bat

NANA RABBIT under an umbrella

A refreshing **PADDLING POOL**

A **FAWN** helping the others stay cool

Fourteen different **HATS**

A mostly hidden **MOUSE**

A speedy **PICNIC BASKET**

A **HANDSTAND** and two **CARTWHEELS**

Three friends making **DAISY CHAINS**

An **ICE CREAM** stand

PUTTING ON A PLAY

I love the atmosphere and sound
of speeches and instructions,
as our animal theater group
prepares the next production!

The play is quite a famous one,
by Shakespeare: full of dreams,
with love and laughter, magic spells,
a fairy king and queen.

Some animals like nothing more
than dressing up to act:
the thrill of playing someone else,
the thrill of hearing claps!

Others star behind the scenes
and help in different ways:
making costumes, painting sets,
and dressing up the stage.

What to spot in the play

- BEAR and WEASEL helping the stars to twinkle
- The FAIRY KING and FAIRY QUEEN wearing handmade crowns
- GRANDPA TOAD making tickets, with a little help from his friends
- MAMA FOX and MAMA WEASEL painting
- A not-very-fierce LION
- Two BUNNIES walking on stilts
- SPIDER spinning a silken spell

NANA RABBIT and PAPA RACCOON
making costumes

A FOX CUB with a bottle of magic potion

MAMA MOUSE directing the play from a
great height

A GRIN and a FROWN

PROFESSOR OWL decorating
the theater

MAMA SQUIRREL and PAPA MOUSE
offering refreshments to cast and crew

PAPA BEAR wearing donkey's ears

Two CATERPILLARS
munching on berries

A loud BAND making an entrance

AUTUMN BRINGS SHORTER DAYS
GOODBYE PARTY

The season's on the turn again,
there's sharpness in the sky.
The leaves are shivering into gold,
the sun is not so high.

But though the year is winding down,
the mood in here is merry,
for there's a sweet and sour feast
of acorns, apples, berries.

Yet there's a note of sadness, too:
Our friend must leave today.
We'll eat and talk and wave,
as we send Chiffchaff on his way.

The woods been home for many months,
this shady, dappled corner.
But now he feels the cold draw near,
he must fly somewhere warmer.

GOODBYE SEE YOU
NEXT YEAR

What to spot at the goodbye party

- **BEAR** taking a rest on **PAPA BEAR**
- A **GIFT** from some of the young animals
- Red, white, and yellow **POPPIES**
- Five **TAILS** under the tablecloth
- **CHIFFCHAFF**, the guest of honor, enjoying the party
- A garland of red **HAWTHORN BERRIES**
- Two **SQUIRRELS** burying acorns
- **PAPA MOUSE** telling a very funny joke
- **MAMA WEASEL** lost in a book
- A **FOX CUB** and a **FAWN** taking a break from the bustle of the party
- The members of the **WOODLAND BAND**
- A cake decorated with juicy **BLACKBERRIES**
- Seven red-and-white **TOADSTOOLS**

RAINY DAY

The rain is pouring down today,
each drop a splashy thud.
The grassy, earthy woodland floor
is now a sea of mud.

A group of damp explorers
have set out to brave the skies,
to jump and stamp in puddles
and make sticky brown mud pies.

Some, like me, have stayed inside:
We do not wish our toes
or tails or fur to ooze with mud,
we'd rather chat or doze.

And other friends are dreamy,
watching drops of liquid light,
which glimmer on the leaves
and make the cloudy wood seem bright.

What to spot on a rainy day

- **BEAR** catching a leak
- Seven **SNAILS** having fun in the rain
- An upside-down **NEST** being used for shelter
- **SPIDER'S WEB** draped in diamonds
- **BEETLES** with leafy umbrellas
- **PAPA SKUNK** snoozing in a hollow tree
- **FROG, TOAD,** and **MICE** jumping into puddles
- **BUNNIES** splashing each other
- **WEASELS** and **RACCOON** making mud pies
- The **DEER FAMILY** with a bowl of apples
- **SNAKE, BEAR'S LITTLE BROTHER,** and **BAT** gazing at raindrops
- Red-orange **ROSE HIPS**
- **MAMA WOODPECKER** and **PROFESSOR OWL** enjoying hot chocolate

ART CLASS

The sharpness in the air
creates a feeling hard to name.
The trees are orange, scarlet, gold,
each leaf a tongue of flame.

And living in this autumn world,
which glows inside the heart,
inspires my friends and I to try
our paws at works of art.

Each artist dreams of building up
their own unique creation,
and fills the paper, clay, or cloth
with wild imagination.

Each piece is different from the next:
the colors, styles, and scenes,
and how it makes you feel inside
and what you think it means.

ART
EXHIBITION

What to spot during art class

- BEAR dreaming up ideas for his next piece of art
- RED ADMIRAL BUTTERFLY being a model for the day
- A bowl of FRUIT and NUTS
- FOX CUBS painting a picture with their paws
- NANA RABBIT admiring BUNNY's drawing
- BEAR'S LITTLE SISTER preparing to start again
- A sculpture made of TWIGS
- RACCOON crafting a special jug
- MICE with needles and thread
- FROG painting a vase of flowers
- A multicolored SKUNK
- WOODPECKER's beak in an unusual place
- The DEER FAMILY posing for a portrait

BEAR'S CAMPFIRE

Against the velvet of the sky,
the fire's a leap of light:
a sun that's settled on the earth,
a hypnotizing sight.

We huddle round the swaying flames
for tales and roasted treats.
We talk and sing and warm our paws
with chestnuts, hot and sweet.

For Owl and Bat, it's daytime now,
and they are wide awake:
each creature swoops among the stars,
a smoky, ghostly shape.

But other friends are getting tired:
it's nearly time for bed.
And round the campfire, there are many
bobbing . . . nodding . . . heads.

What to spot at Bear's campfire

- **BEAR** telling a thrilling campfire story
- Two **MOLES** perched on their molehills
- A pile of **SWEET CHESTNUTS** ready for roasting
- Three swooping **BATS**
- **FROG** taking a bath to keep cool
- **TOAD** hidden under a pile of leaves
- **SPIDER**'s golden web
- **RACCOONS** and **MICE** enjoying the warmth
- **FAWN** playing the fiddle
- **BIRDS** resting in the trees
- **PROFESSOR OWL** wide awake
- Three sleeping **SKUNKS**
- **MAMA FOX** dancing with her **CUBS**
- Five **FIREFLIES**
- A glowing **CRESCENT MOON**

WINTER BRINGS THE COLD
WINTER SPORTS

The sun is lower in the sky
and many trees are bare.
The snowflakes spiral silently
through peaceful silver air.

The wood is not so quiet, though:
it rings with rowdy glee.
We've all met up, with chattering teeth,
to sled and skate and ski.

We teeter, totter, twirl, and glide,
make angels in the snow.
We slide around the icy trees
and dodge the mistletoe.

And when our toes are truly cold,
we gulp a steaming drink.
Then out again to seize the day
before the sun can sink!

What to spot during winter sports

- **BEAR** skating on a frozen pond
- A **RACE** through the wintry branches
- Skiing **SKUNKS**
- Three **SNOW ANGELS**
- **MICE** tangled up in a ball of mistletoe
- A **SNOWBALL FIGHT**
- Eight branches dripping with **ICICLES**
- **MAMA FOX** stuck in the snow
- Three **SQUIRRELS** searching for and digging up acorns
- A **SNOW DEER**
- **BUNNIES** piled onto a sled
- Red **HOLLY BERRIES** and black **IVY BERRIES**
- The **PIGEON FAMILY** making footprints in the snow

BEAR'S WINTER FEAST

In the depths of wintertime,
a feast is just the thing
to raise our chilly spirits,
with a chance to eat and sing!

We've gathered sprigs of holly
to make ruby-studded wreaths,
and garlanded the empty boughs
with green and russet leaves.

Around the heaving tables
sit a heap of happy guests.
We're sharing songs of snow and fire,
and merry yarns, and jests.

The winter sun is setting fast:
It never reached full height.
But we will linger on here
in this jolly, joyful night.

What to spot at Bear's winter feast

- BEAR wearing a leaf and berry crown
- Four HOLLY WREATHS
- Three MICE performing in special costumes
- BUNNY, FAWN, and a FOX CUB making garlands
- RACCOONS and MICE greeting their visitors
- A game of DOMINOS
- PAPA DEER's decorated antlers

TEAMS

A nearly completed **JIGSAW PUZZLE**

A **PUPPET** show

A book of **SONGS**

An indoor **BOWLING ALLEY**

CHIPMUNK perching on a pie

A **MAP** of the woods

A very hungry **SKUNK**

The winter **SUN** low in the sky

The **SQUIRREL FAMILY** being generous with their acorns

GOODNIGHT WORLD
BEAR'S DEN

The year is getting *sleepy* now,
the *night* is getting on.
    It's way beyond my *bedtime:*
do excuse this giant *yawn!*

Everyone has said *goodnight,*
sleep tight, and *see you soon.*
And now I'm in my *cozy den*
beneath the gentle *moon.*

I plan to *sleep,* like many friends,
until the start of *spring,*
dozing through the frozen weeks
that *frosty winter* brings.

The year will *wake* again, in time,
to *warmer, brighter* skies.
But now we need to *rest* and *dream,*
so *shhh* and *close your eyes.*

What to spot in Bear's den

- **BEAR** cuddling his teddy
- A patchwork **BLANKET** to snuggle under
- A **SNOW GLOBE** placed on the shelf
- Shelves full of **BOOKS**
- Bunk beds full of **BUNNIES**
- Yellow-striped **PAJAMAS**
- Camouflaged **SNAIL SHELLS**
- A snuffed-out **CANDLE**
- Fluffy **SKUNK TAILS** poking out of their den
- A hammock full of cozy **CHIPMUNKS**
- Four **BATS** sleeping peacefully upside-down
- Two toy **RABBITS** tucked close to their owners
- Two **MOLES** dozing inside their molehill
- **SNAKE** snoring in the root of a tree
- Rows of resting **BIRDS**
- **PROFESSOR OWL** watching over her friends

NATURE TRAIL

These nature inspired illustrations were hidden in Bear's world. Did you spot them?

Turn back the pages and revisit the woodland to try to find them.

Nature is everywhere. It's up in the air, under the ground and all around us. We only need to look. Here are some ideas for you to explore and get creative outside . . .

SPRING BRINGS NEW LIFE

Birds singing

The longer, lighter days of spring encourage male birds to start singing in their quest to find a partner. Each species of bird has a unique song—sit quietly outside one morning and tune into how many different calls you can hear. Ask an adult to help you write down the sounds of their songs—you'll probably end up with some unusual letter combinations!

Flowering trees

Many trees flower in spring. Sometimes the flowers are eye-catching, like this pretty pink blossom. But sometimes you have to look more closely at the tree to see them. Can you find three different types of flowering trees? What color are their flowers?

Tree stump

Tree stumps are often full of life. Even new trees can grow from a stump! Next time you come across one, take a good look. You might not see a woodland school—but are there any insects, plants, or fungi?

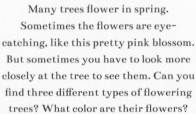

Nests

Lots of birds build their nests in spring. Some birds will only have one egg, and others can have as many as fifteen! Look up into the trees around you—can you spot any twiggy, grassy nests?

Burrows

Rabbits create burrows underground. Next time you're out and about, look for telltale holes dug in the earth—there might be someone living underneath your feet! Make up a name for them, and tell someone a short story about what they're doing right now.

Creepy-crawlies

Ants, caterpillars, crickets, woodlice, ladybugs and bees are all arthropods—this means their skeleton is on the outside and their body is made of segments. Look at all the different shapes and colors! Go outside and pay close attention— can you see or hear one of these little creatures? Will it stay in one place long enough for you to draw it?

Leaf shapes

Leaves come in varied shapes, sizes, and forms. Some are glossy, and some are hairy. Some are long and thin like needles, and some are shaped a bit like stars. Some are smooth at the edges, and some have jagged teeth. Collect as many differently shaped fallen leaves as you can find, then present your own science show, holding up and describing your favorite leaves.

Flying insects

Is there a pond, lake, or river near you? Then there are probably hundreds of flying insects! They are so light and lacy, it's often easy to miss them. Sit quietly for a few minutes, looking around and over the water. Can you spot the largest and the smallest flying insects?

Rough bark

Each species of tree has a particular type of bark: shiny, rough, light, dark, striped, scaly . . . Bark is satisfying to touch. Close your eyes and press your hands gently against different trees. Can you think of a word to describe how they feel? You might like to take out some paper and pencils to make bark rubbings.

Fruit in season

Different fruits grow at different times of the year. Next time you're at the store or the market, ask someone who works there which fruits are in season—this generally means they'll be grown in the area where you live.

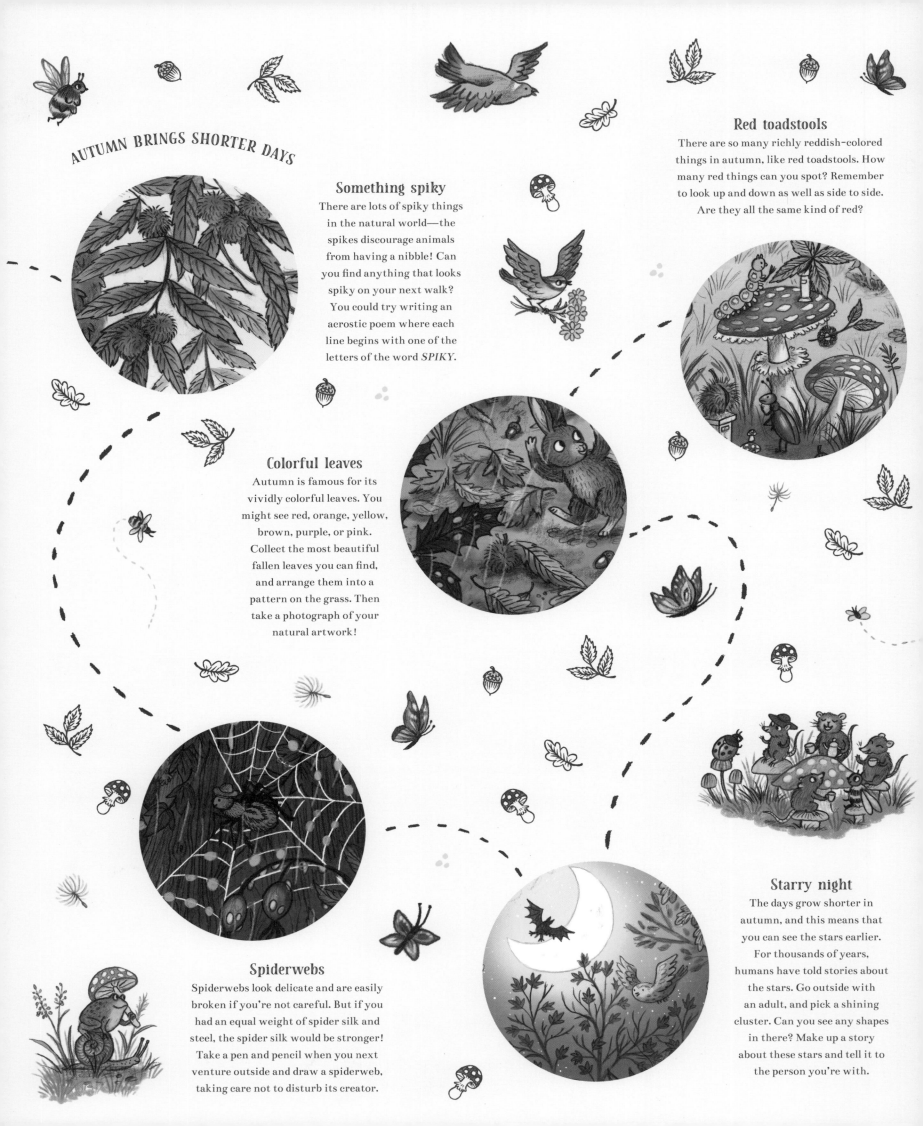

Something spiky

There are lots of spiky things in the natural world—the spikes discourage animals from having a nibble! Can you find anything that looks spiky on your next walk? You could try writing an acrostic poem where each line begins with one of the letters of the word *SPIKY*.

Red toadstools

There are so many richly reddish-colored things in autumn, like red toadstools. How many red things can you spot? Remember to look up and down as well as side to side. Are they all the same kind of red?

Colorful leaves

Autumn is famous for its vividly colorful leaves. You might see red, orange, yellow, brown, purple, or pink. Collect the most beautiful fallen leaves you can find, and arrange them into a pattern on the grass. Then take a photograph of your natural artwork!

Spiderwebs

Spiderwebs look delicate and are easily broken if you're not careful. But if you had an equal weight of spider silk and steel, the spider silk would be stronger! Take a pen and pencil when you next venture outside and draw a spiderweb, taking care not to disturb its creator.

Starry night

The days grow shorter in autumn, and this means that you can see the stars earlier. For thousands of years, humans have told stories about the stars. Go outside with an adult, and pick a shining cluster. Can you see any shapes in there? Make up a story about these stars and tell it to the person you're with.

Clouds

If the weather is cold and the air is not too dry, your breath can make a white cloud as you breathe out. This is the natural water vapor in your breath turning into tiny droplets of water or ice as it hits the air. Have fun making cloud shapes the next time the weather is cold!

Bare trees

Trees that lose their leaves in winter are called deciduous. They make beautiful silhouettes against the winter sky. Pick your favorite bare trees and try to imitate their shape with your body.

Acorns ahoy!

Squirrels bury nuts in autumn, to dig up and eat in the winter when it's harder to find food. Have you seen any squirrels scrabbling up buried treats near you? What about other wild animals who are active in winter—what do they eat?

Animal tracks

Have you ever woken up to a blanket of snow, punctured by crisp animal footprints? It's an amazing sight! If you look closely at muddy or frosty ground, you might be able to see some tracks there as well. Examine the size and shape. Can you guess which animal made them?

The moon

Our glowing moon looks like different shapes all the time. A new moon is invisible, then it grows in size—waxes—until it's full, and then decreases in size—wanes—until it's invisible again. If you look outside over the course of a month, you will see these changes in the sky above you. Which is your favorite shape?

NATURE RESOURCES

If you'd like to find out more about the natural world, here are some suggested sites for you to explore with an adult.

American Forests
A nonprofit conservation organization working to protect and restore forests in the United States. A great resource for learning more about climate change, wildlife, and social equity through conservation.

americanforests.org

Audubon for Kids
This gorgeous website brings the bird world closer, with facts, games, art ideas, and other activities.

audubon.org/get-outside/activities/audubon-for-kids

Brooklyn Botanic Garden
One of the largest botanic gardens in New York, the Brooklyn Botanic Gardens offer educational resources, activities, gardening resources, and even photos of the plants currently in bloom in their gardens.

bbg.org

The Conversation for Kids–Seasons
This smart website takes questions from kids and answers them thoroughly and thoughtfully. Here, two scientists answer a question about the seasons.

theconversation.com/curious-kids-why-are-there-different -seasons-at-specific-times-of-the-year-109380

Defenders of Wildlife
This conservation organization aims to protect wildlife across North America. Wander around their website to learn more about North American plants and animals and their hugely different habitats.

defenders.org

The Kids Should See This
This is a beautiful time-lapse video of a forest in Indiana over the seasons. Watch it when you feel like taking the time to slow down.

thekidshouldseethis.com/post/a-forest-year

National Geographic Kids
Animal facts, quizzes, interviews, and some wonderful photographs make this a rich resource.

natgeokids.com

The Wildlife Trust
As well as being packed with fascinating information on different species, this site has a series of live camera feeds, offering an exciting up-close look at the lives of owls, ospreys, puffins, and many others!

wildlifetrusts.org

POETRY RESOURCES

If you'd like to find out more about poems and poetry, here are some suggested sites for you to explore with an adult.

The Children's Poetry Archive
This is a treasure trove of audio recordings of poems. Hearing a poet read their own work really brings it to life. You can search by theme and age, and you'll get a special peek into how and why the poets wrote their poems.

childrens.poetryarchive.org/

Poetry 180
Set up by U.S. poet laureate Billy Collins, Poetry 180 makes it easy for children to hear or read a poem each day of the 180 days of the school year.

loc.gov/poetry/180

The Poetry Foundation
The American Poetry Foundation has a wealth of children's poems, as well as some magical poem films.

poetryfoundation.org/learn/children

Poetry Minute
Created by U.S. Children's Poet Laureate Kenn Nesbitt, each of the poems on this website can be read in about one minute and the site provides a new poem for each day of the school year.

poetryminute.org

Poetry Out Loud
With plenty of poets and collections to browse, these poems can be performed out loud, shared with others, or simply read in your head.

poetryoutloud.org

The Poetry Society
The U.K. Poetry Society has a great website called Poetry Class, with poetry lessons and activities on a whole variety of themes. These resources will guide you through writing your very own poem!

resources.poetrysociety.org.uk

Poets.org
A wonderful website that includes poems to read, more information about the Academy of American Poets and National Poetry Month, and a glossary of poetic terms.

poets.org

Reading Rockets
This website, dedicated to developing young readers, has loads of poetry resources—just type *poetry* into the search box and you'll find countless inspiring ideas!

readingrockets.org